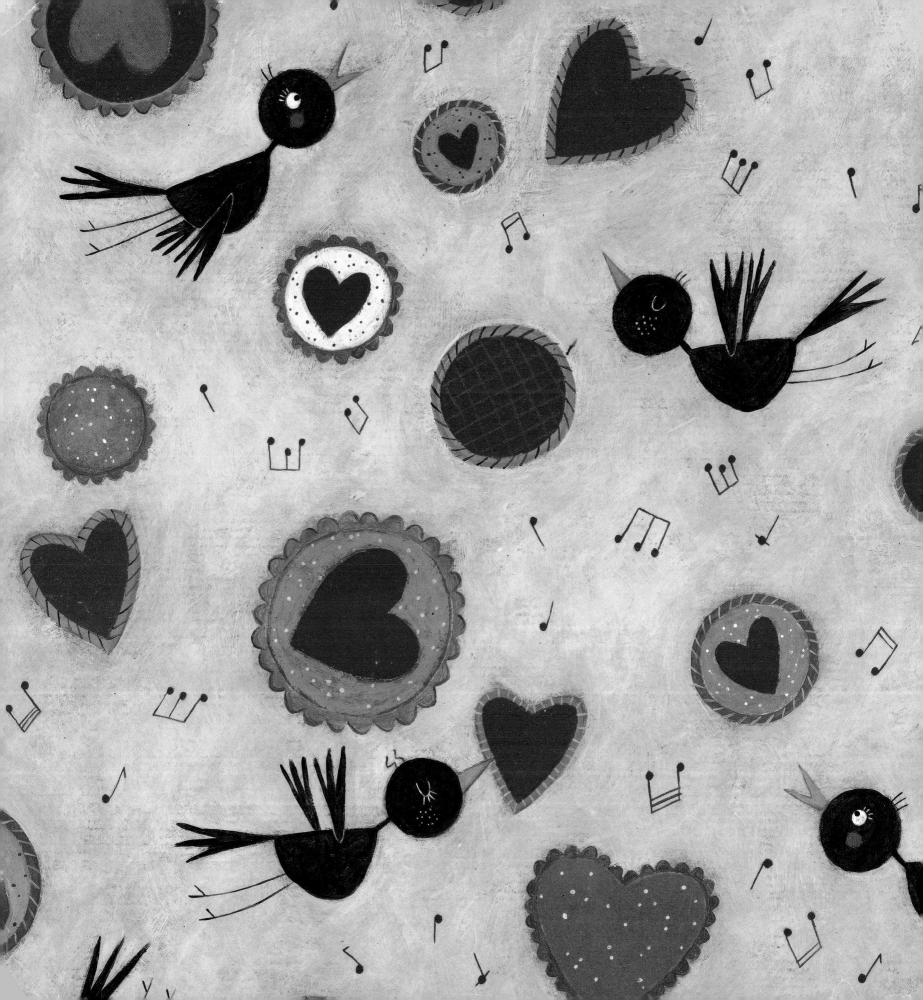

For Bernie with all my love. D.C

For Gran and Aunt Nora - you'd have loved this! M.W

THE GREAT NURSERY RHYME DISASTER

First published in hardback in 2008
This paperback edition first published in 2010
by Hodder Children's Books

Text copyright © David Conway 2008
Illustrations copyright © Melanie Williamson 2008

Hodder Children's Books
338 Euston Road
London NW1 3BH

Hodder Children's Books Australia
Level 17/207 Kent Street
Sydney, NSW 2000

ISBN: 978 0 340 94508 7

Printed in China

Hodder Children's Books
is a division of Hachette Children's Books.
An Hachette UK Company.
www.hachette.co.uk

THE GREAT NURSERY RHYME DISASTER

WRITTEN BY
DAVID CONWAY

ILLUSTRATED BY
MELANIE WILLIAMSON

Hodder Children's Books

A division of Hachette Children's Books

LITTLE MISS MUFFET WAS BORED.

She was bored of being in the same
old nursery rhyme and she'd had
quite enough of that scary,
little spider.

'What I need,'
she told herself,
'is a change.'

So off she went into
the pages of the book
to find another nursery
rhyme to be in.

Along the way she met the Grand Old Duke
of York. 'May I be in your rhyme?' asked Little
Miss Muffet, politely.

'Of course!' said the Duke, 'GET IN LINE!'

OH, THE GRAND OLD DUKE OF YORK,
HE HAD TEN THOUSAND MEN.
HE MARCHED THEM AND MISS MUFFET UP
TO THE TOP OF THE HILL,
AND HE MARCHED THEM ALL DOWN AGAIN.

'Oh, no!' complained Miss Muffet.
'There's far too much marching for my liking.'
And with that she toddled off into the pages
of the book to find a better rhyme to be in.

NEXT
RHYME

Soon after, she saw Jack and Jill going up a hill.
They were happy to let Little Miss Muffet
try out their rhyme…

JACK AND JILL AND MISS MUFFET
WENT UP THE HILL,
TO FETCH A PAIL OF WATER;
MISS MUFFET FELL DOWN
AND BROKE HER CROWN,
AND JACK AND JILL
CAME TUMBLING AFTER.

'This nursery rhyme is much too painful,'
cried Little Miss Muffet, hobbling off to find
a rhyme that didn't hurt so much.

SMELLY
CHEESE

On the next page, Little Miss Muffet spotted a mouse by an old grandfather clock. 'May I be in your rhyme?' she asked.

'Marvellous!' said the mouse. 'I'm tired of scurrying up and down that clock.'

HICKORY, DICKORY, DOCK,
MISS MUFFET CLIMBED
UP THE CLOCK.
THE CLOCK STRUCK ONE,
MISS MUFFET SLID DOWN,
HICKORY, DICKORY, DOCK.

'I look ridiculous!' said Little Miss Muffet as her cheeks turned almost purple with embarrassment.

And with that she sneaked off to find a rhyme that didn't make her look quite so silly.

NAUGHTY BOYS

Further on, Little Miss Muffet met Johnny Flynn and little Tommy Stout. The two boys giggled to each other as they let her try out their rhyme...

DING, DONG, BELL, MISS MUFFET'S IN THE WELL. WHO PUT HER IN? LITTLE JOHNNY FLYNN. WHO PULLED HER OUT? LITTLE TOMMY STOUT.

A very wet Miss Muffet **screamed** and ran to the next page of the book as fast as she could to find a rhyme that had no naughty boys in it!

JUMPING COW

It wasn't long before Little Miss Muffet ran into a dish and a spoon. 'May I be in your rhyme?' she asked.

'Yes, you can play the part of the dish!' said the cow.

HEY DIDDLE, DIDDLE,
THE CAT AND THE FIDDLE,
THE COW JUMPED OVER THE MOON;
THE LITTLE DOG LAUGHED TO SEE SUCH FUN
AND MISS MUFFET RAN AWAY WITH THE SPOON.

I ♥ DOG

'Splendid!' said the cow.
But the dish wasn't happy
and a terrible rumpus broke out
all over the page…

'I'LL HAVE YOU KNOW THAT I'VE BEEN RUNNING AWAY WITH THAT SPOON EVER SINCE THIS RHYME WAS WRITTEN!' screamed the dish.

FOLLOW FOR
BLACKBIRD PIES

The **rumpus** spilled over onto the next page...

and then the next...

The Queen of Hearts **wasn't** making
tarts anymore, but Incy Wincy Spider was.

Mary **didn't** have a little lamb,
but instead was followed
by Three Blind Mice.

And it **wasn't** Humpty Dumpty falling off the wall, but Old Mother Hubbard!

While all this was going on Little Miss Muffet, who by now had decided that she no longer needed a change, tiptoed quietly back through the pages of the book, and returned to her very own rhyme.

But she soon remembered why she had wanted a change in the first place!

Little Miss Muffet sat on a tuffet,
Eating her curds and whey;
Along came a spider,
Who sat down beside her
And frightened Miss Muffet away.

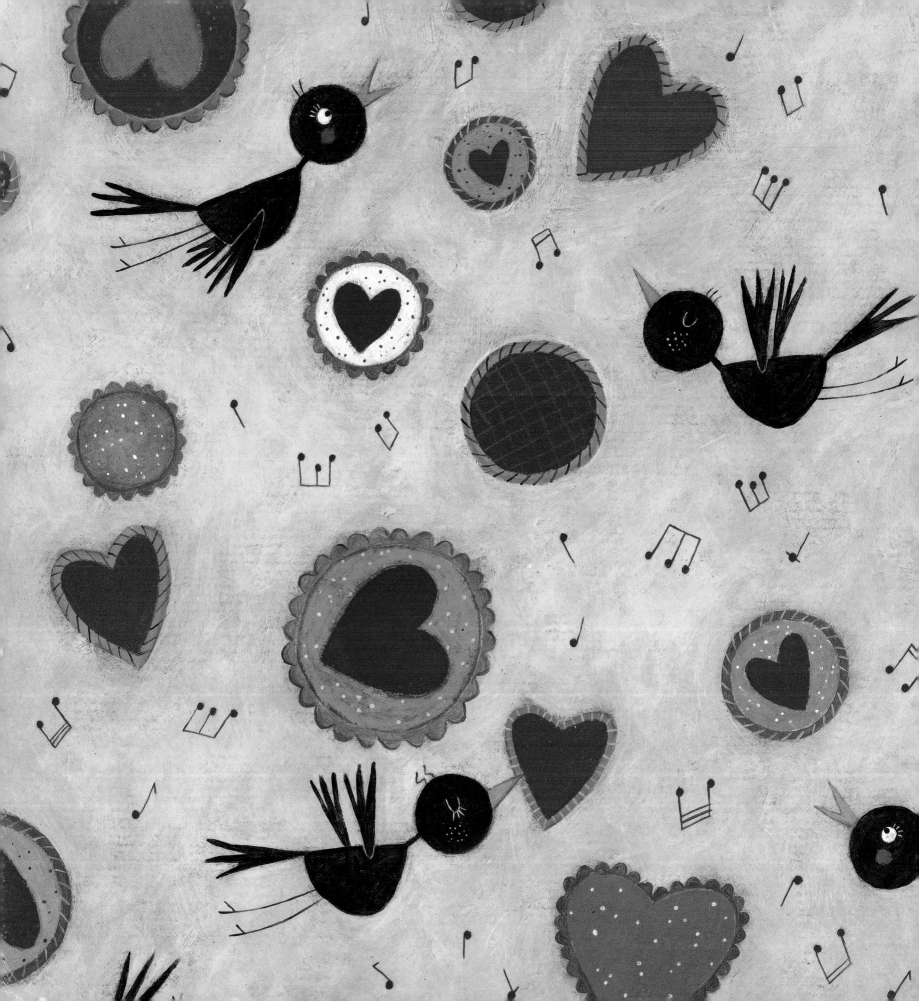

Other great Hodder picture books perfect to share with children:

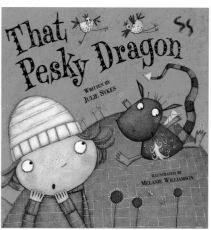

978 0 340 91161 7 (PB)

978 0 340 93200 1 (PB)

978 0 340 91153 2 (PB)

978 0 340 95059 3 (HB)
978 0 340 95060 9 (PB)

978 0 340 93083 0 (HB)
978 0 340 93084 7 (PB)

Hodder
Children's
Books

A division of Hachette Children's Books